MW00930923

In loving memory of:
Joel D. Namy
&
Karen A. Namy

www.mascotbooks.com

Lakeside Friends: A Story About Cancer

©2022 Anne Bramlage. All Rights Reserved. No part of this publication may be reproduced, stored in a retrieval system or transmitted in any form by any means electronic, mechanical, or photocopying, recording or otherwise without the permission of the author.

For more information, please contact:
Mascot Books
620 Herndon Parkway, Suite 320
Herndon, VA 20170
info@mascotbooks.com

Library of Congress Control Number: 2021912091

CPSIA Code: PRT0921A
ISBN-13: 978-1-64543-597-6

Printed in the United States

KARIS & BROOK STORIES

Lakeside Friends
A Story About Cancer

A. B. Namy

Illustrated by Agus Prajogo and Yohanes Bastian

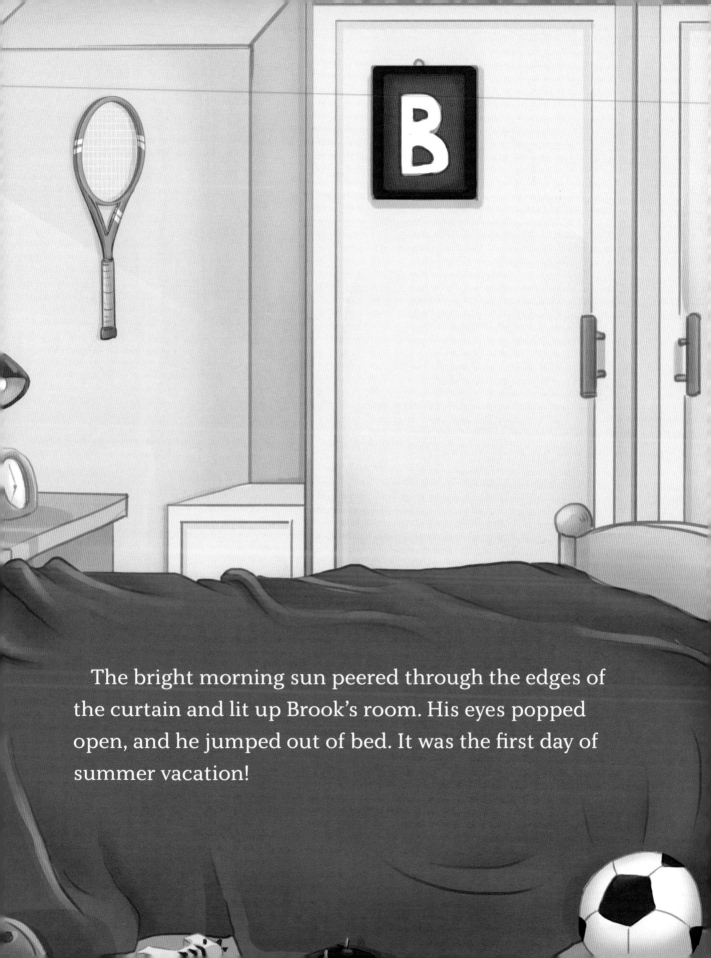

The bright morning sun peered through the edges of the curtain and lit up Brook's room. His eyes popped open, and he jumped out of bed. It was the first day of summer vacation!

Brook rushed downstairs, skipping the last step as he turned the corner and headed into the kitchen.

"Well, good morning, honey!" his mom said.

"Good morning, Mom," he replied as he reached for a bowl in the cupboard.

While he poured himself a bowl of cereal, he asked, "Mom, can we go to the lake today? I want to go swimming with Joel."

"That's a great idea," she said. "I will call Joel's mom to see if he can join us. But before we leave, we have a few chores to do around the house. Would you please clean your room and then sweep the front porch?"

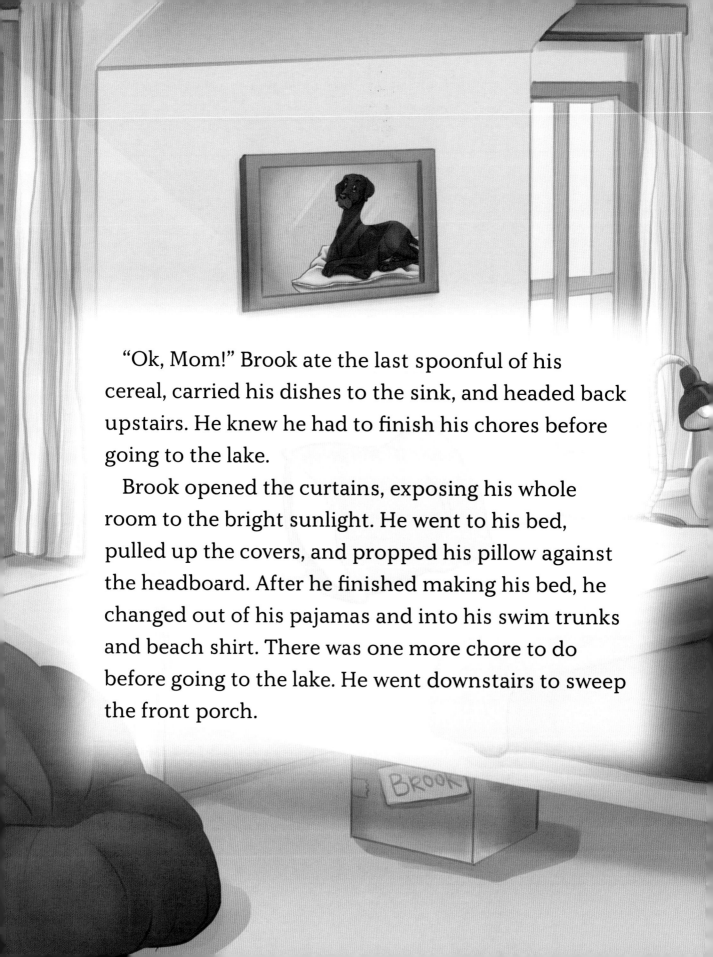

"Ok, Mom!" Brook ate the last spoonful of his cereal, carried his dishes to the sink, and headed back upstairs. He knew he had to finish his chores before going to the lake.

Brook opened the curtains, exposing his whole room to the bright sunlight. He went to his bed, pulled up the covers, and propped his pillow against the headboard. After he finished making his bed, he changed out of his pajamas and into his swim trunks and beach shirt. There was one more chore to do before going to the lake. He went downstairs to sweep the front porch.

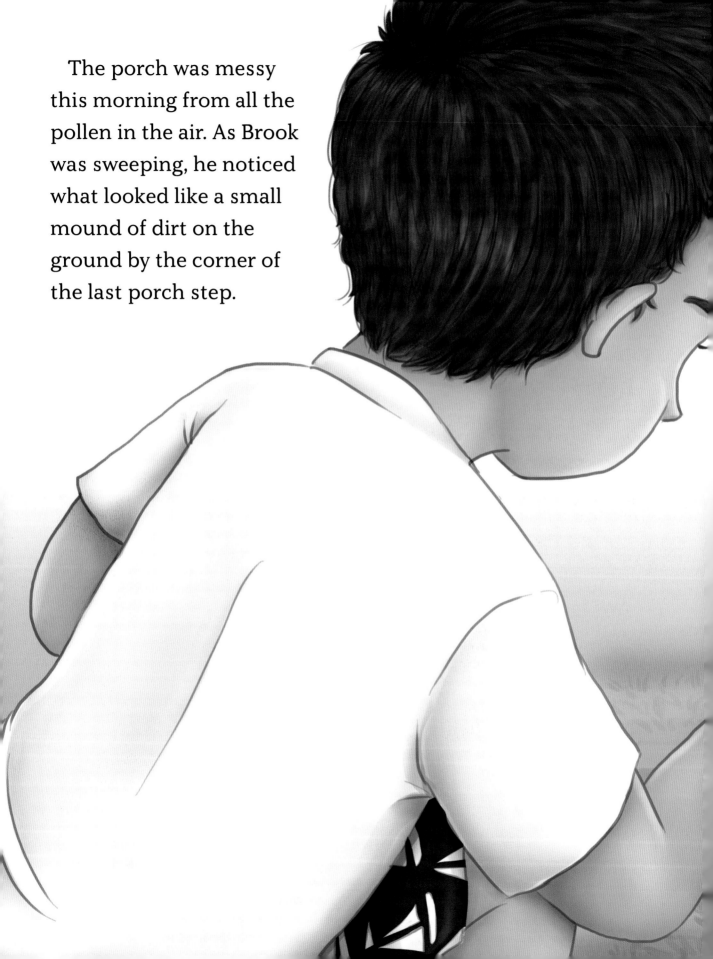

The porch was messy this morning from all the pollen in the air. As Brook was sweeping, he noticed what looked like a small mound of dirt on the ground by the corner of the last porch step.

Brook bent down to take a closer look and saw ants crawling in and out of a hole on top of the little hill. He ran inside to get his magnifying glass to have a better look.

Brook saw four ants in a row carrying an object as they returned to the hill. He then saw another ant crawling out of the hole with a brown piece of dirt. Just a few inches away from these, he saw three more ants gathering more dirt, and next to the anthill was a small puddle where a few ants were getting water.

Just then, Brook's mom came outside. "Almost time to go!" she announced.

He finished sweeping, grabbed his bag, and headed for the car.

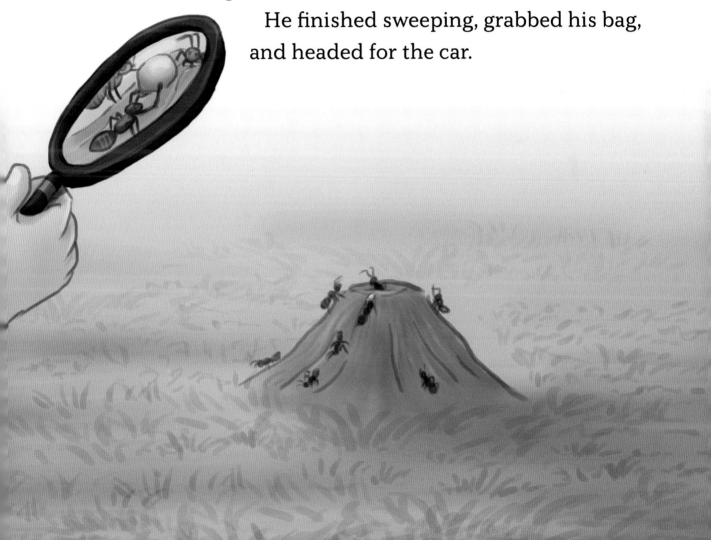

Brook's mom started the car, and they headed to the lake. On the way, Brook began thinking about the ants and how each ant was doing something different. *They must be doing jobs that make the anthill larger,* Brook thought.

"We're here." His mom's voice interrupted Brook's thoughts. Brook forgot all about the ants and looked toward the lake, where he saw his cousin, Karis, playing in the sand. "Here, Mom, take the bag, please. I want to go play with Karis." He jumped out of the car.

After a while, Brook noticed that Joel hadn't arrived. He walked over to his mom and asked politely, "When is Joel coming?"

His mom replied sadly, "I just got off the phone with Joel's mom, and he will not be able to come to the lake today. He's not feeling very well."

Brook was disappointed that he would not be able to swim with Joel, but he figured Joel could come another day. Brook went back to building sand castles with Karis.

Early the next morning, the phone rang. It was Joel's mom asking if Brook wanted to get ice cream with Joel after lunch that day.

"Okay, that sounds like fun—we will meet you there," said Brook's mom as she hung up the phone. "Brook, we are going to meet Joel for ice cream in town after lunch," she said. Brook was so excited to see Joel.

As they were leaving the house, Brook looked down at the anthill he had seen the day before. "Look, Mom, the anthill is getting bigger," Brook said.

"Yes, it is," his mom replied. "Each ant has a job to do, and when every ant does their job, the colony grows."

Brook took a step back and thought, *Every ant has a job, like getting food, water, and dirt for the anthill. And I clean my room and sweep the porch—I have jobs, too.*

"WOW," said Brook, and he wondered, *What would happen to the ants if some of them didn't do their jobs any longer?*

Brook saw Joel from a distance as they neared the ice cream shop. "Hi, Joel!" yelled Brook.

"Hi Brook," Joel called back. As they gave each other a high-five, Brook noticed there was something different about Joel. Brook wasn't sure what it was. *Joel is wearing a baseball cap, but he always wears hats,* Brook thought to himself. *So that's not it.*

Then Brook figured it out: "Joel, what happened to your hair?" he asked. Brook could tell that Joel's hair was shorter than he had ever seen.

"Oh, I thought it would be cool to have shorter hair for the summer," Joel replied.

"I like it!" Brook said. "Maybe I'll get a buzz cut for the summer, too." The two boys sat on a bench and enjoyed their ice cream cones together.

On the walk home, Brook asked his mom if he could get a buzz cut just like Joel so he could stay cool in the summer, too. "We'll see," his mom said.

When they got home, Brook's mom stopped at the front steps and gestured for them to sit together. "Honey, do you remember how Joel couldn't go to the lake yesterday?" she asked Brook.

"Yes, because he wasn't feeling well," Brook answered.

"That's right, Brook. You see, Joel is sick," she said.

"But not sick like a cold. Joel has cancer, and he is taking medicine that makes his hair fall out. He couldn't come to the lake because he would be exposed to too many germs, and germs could make him feel worse," Mom added.

"What's cancer?" Brook asked.

"Cancer is uncontrolled cell growth. Everyone has cells in their body, and every cell has a job to make your body function. Cancer starts when cells don't do their jobs," his mom explained. "Uncontrolled cells are cells that are growing in number and are not doing their designated job. This is what's causing Joel's body to be sick."

"What do you mean they don't want to do their jobs?" Brook looked confused.

Brook's mom looked down at the anthill. "Look at your anthill here. Do you see every ant working?" she asked.

Brook exclaimed, "Yes!"

"Well, suppose the ants that gathered food did not want to do their job anymore."

"That would be bad," Brook answered.

"You're right, Brook, and why would it be bad?" she asked.

"I've been thinking about that," Brook responded. "I'm not really sure."

"If the ants don't do what they are supposed to do, it can hurt the whole colony," she explained.

"Are all my cells working?" Brook asked.

His mom looked at him and smiled. "Yes, your cells are all working just fine."

Brook looked at his mom and smiled back. "I want to make something special for my friend Joel," he said as he leaned over to whisper it in her ear.

His mom smiled and said, "Great idea. He will love it!"

After breakfast the next morning, Brook asked his mom for a large Mason jar. "Can Karis come to the lake as well?" he added.

"Sure," Mom said.

When it was time to go to the lake that afternoon, Brook brought the jar with them. Brook carried the jar to the sand and started to shovel some sand into the bottom of the jar.

"What are you doing?" asked Karis.

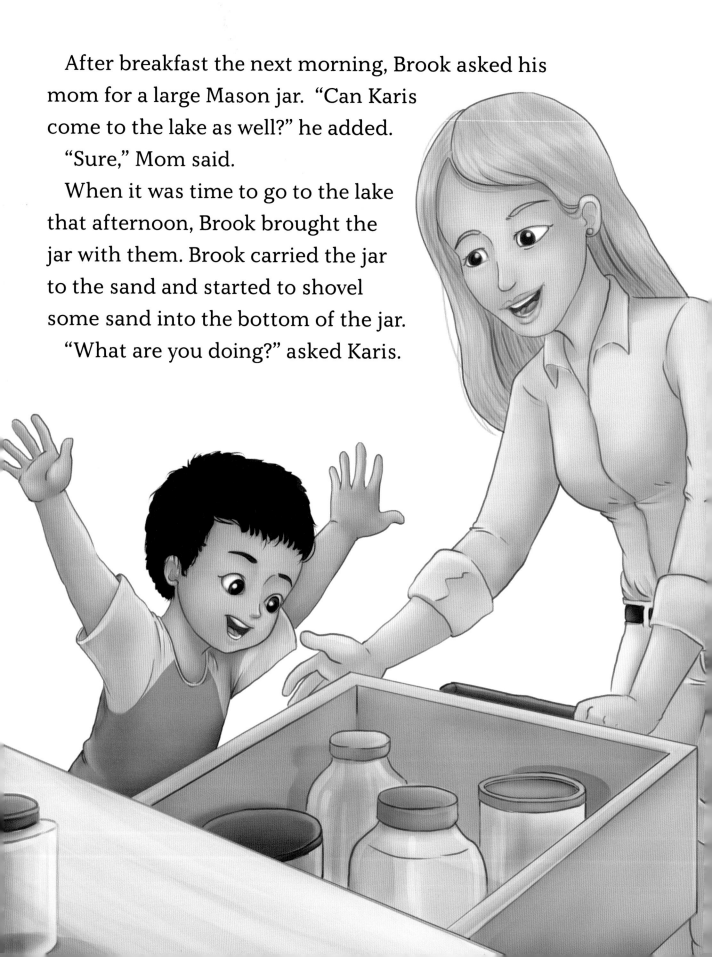

"I'm making something for Joel! Would you like to help?" Brook asked.

"Yeah, sure!" Karis was so happy to help her older cousin. The two worked hard on Joel's surprise.

On the way home from the lake, Brook and his mom stopped at Joel's house to give him the surprise. Brook got out of the car and went up to the front door.

Joel's mom opened the door, and Brook smiled at her. "Hi, I'm wondering if Joel is here? I brought him a gift."

"Yes, he is on the couch in the family room," she said.

Brook went to the family room. "Hi, Joel!" he said. Joel was reading a book.

Joel sat up and smiled. "Hi, Brook. What's up?"

Brook walked over and handed him the Mason jar. "Here, Joel, I made you something."

Joel looked at the jar. In the bottom of the jar was sand, then some little pebbles, then lake water filled the rest of the jar. "I know you can't come to the lake much this summer, so I brought the lake to you in a jar!" Brook exclaimed. Floating on the water under the lid was a small, yellow rubber duck. "Remember how much fun we had last summer when we fed the ducks?" Brook asked.

Joel enjoyed the lake jar. "Thanks, Brook! I like it a lot! Next summer I can spend every day at the lake with you."

Brook smiled and said, "I can't wait, Joel!" The boys laughed as they tilted the jar back and forth to watch the duck swim.

**With each new day,
Encourage a friend
In a different way.**

About the Author

Dr. Anne Namy Bramlage grew up in Cazenovia, New York, and the small town people and lakeside community are brought to life in the pages of her books.

As a childhood cancer survivor, and now a visually impaired adult, Anne brings real-life experiences to the stories she develops. Combining her passion for education and her interest in storytelling, Anne seeks to enhance awareness of the challenges others face.

You can find Anne with her husband, Justin, and dog, Karis, by the water or walking trails as she works out the next adventure of Karis and Brook!